Growing Readers

Purchased with Smart Start Funds

I Know an Old Lady Who Swallowed a PIE

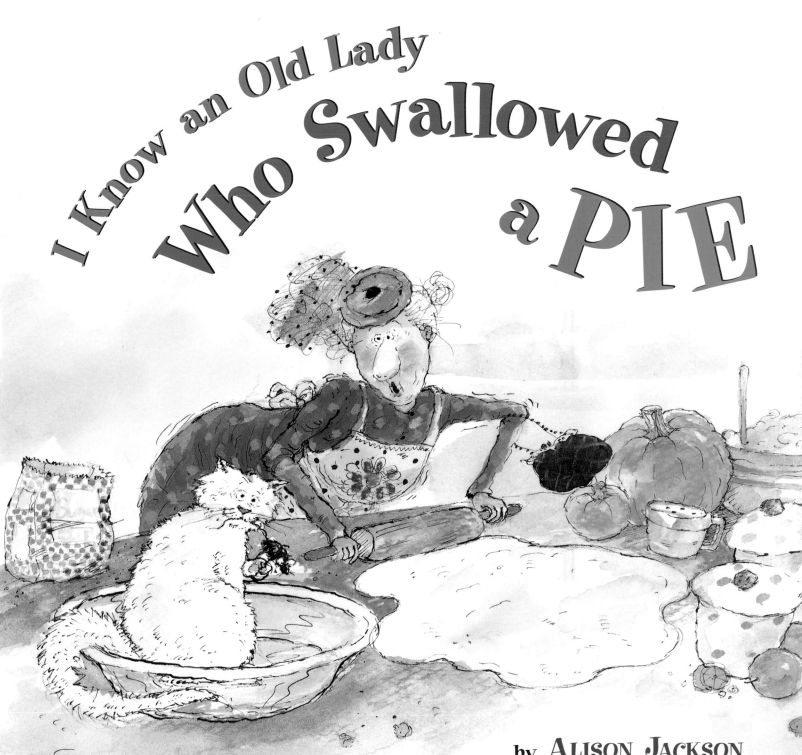

by **ALISON JACKSON**

Pictures by
JUDITH BYRON SCHACHNER

Dutton Children's Books
New York

For Kyle and Quinn, who asked Mom to write something silly
A.J.

For Ted and Kev,
two of the greatest pie-eaters I know,
with love from your crazy sister Jude
J.B.S.

Text copyright © 1997 by Alison Jackson
Illustrations copyright © 1997 by Judith Byron Schachner

CIP Data is available.

Published in the United States 1997 by Dutton Children's Books,
a division of Penguin Books USA Inc.
375 Hudson Street, New York, New York 10014

Designed by Semadar Megged
Printed in Hong Kong   First Edition
ISBN 0-525-45645-7
10 9 8 7 6

I know an old lady

who swallowed a pie,

A THANKSGIVING PIE, WHICH WAS REALLY TOO DRY.

PERHAPS SHE'LL DIE.

I know an old lady who swallowed **some cider**

THAT RUMBLED AND MUMBLED AND GRUMBLED INSIDE HER.

She swallowed the cider to moisten the pie,
The Thanksgiving pie, which was really too dry.

PERHAPS SHE'LL DIE.

I know an old lady who swallowed **a roll.**

Just swallowed it whole—the entire roll!

She swallowed the roll to go with the cider
That rumbled and mumbled and grumbled inside her.

She swallowed the cider to moisten the pie,
The Thanksgiving pie, which was really too dry.

Perhaps she'll die.

I know an old lady who swallowed **a squash.**

OH MY GOSH, A FAT YELLOW SQUASH!

She swallowed the squash to go with the roll.

She swallowed the roll to go with the cider
That rumbled and mumbled and grumbled inside her.

She swallowed the cider to moisten the pie,
The Thanksgiving pie, which was really too dry.

PERHAPS SHE'LL DIE.

I know an old lady who swallowed **a salad.**

SHE WAS LOOKING QUITE PALLID FROM EATING THAT SALAD!

She swallowed the salad to go with the squash.

She swallowed the squash to go with the roll.

She swallowed the roll to go with the cider
That rumbled and mumbled and grumbled inside her.

She swallowed the cider to moisten the pie,
The Thanksgiving pie, which was really too dry.

PERHAPS SHE'LL DIE.

I know an old lady who swallowed **a turkey.**

HER FUTURE LOOKED MURKY, AFTER THAT TURKEY!

She swallowed the turkey to go with the salad.

She swallowed the salad to go with the squash.

She swallowed the squash to go with the roll.

She swallowed the roll to go with the cider
That rumbled and mumbled and grumbled inside her.

She swallowed the cider to moisten the pie,
The Thanksgiving pie, which was really too dry.

PERHAPS SHE'LL DIE.

I know an old lady who swallowed **a pot.**

I KID YOU NOT—SHE SWALLOWED A POT!

She swallowed the pot to go with the turkey.

She swallowed the turkey to go with the salad.

She swallowed the salad to go with the squash.

She swallowed the squash to go with the roll.

She swallowed the roll to go with the cider
That rumbled and mumbled and grumbled inside her.

She swallowed the cider to moisten the pie,
The Thanksgiving pie, which was really too dry.

PERHAPS SHE'LL DIE.

I know an old lady who swallowed **a cake.**

FOR GOODNESS SAKE, A TEN-LAYER CAKE!

She swallowed the cake to go with the pot.

She swallowed the pot to go with the turkey.

She swallowed the turkey to go with the salad.

She swallowed the salad to go with the squash.

She swallowed the squash to go with the roll.

She swallowed the roll to go with the cider
That rumbled and mumbled and grumbled inside her.

She swallowed the cider to moisten the pie,
The Thanksgiving pie, which was really too dry.

PERHAPS SHE'LL DIE.

I know an old lady

who swallowed **some bread.**

"I'M FULL," SHE SAID.

Growing Readers
New Hanover County
Public Library
201 Chestnut Street
Wilmington, NC 28401

BAG BOOK